4/16

To my wonderful friend of more than
forty years, fellow artist, Allan Markman.
—Douglas Florian

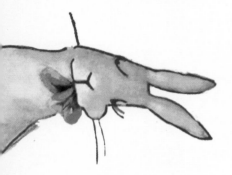

🐝 little bee books

An imprint of Bonnier Publishing Group
853 Broadway, New York, New York 10003
Text copyright © 2016 by Douglas Florian
Illustrations copyright © 2016 by Sonia Sánchez

Manufactured in China LEO 0915
First Edition 10 9 8 7 6 5 4 3 2 1
Library of Congress Cataloging-in-Publication Data
is available upon request.
ISBN 978-1-4998-0104-0
littlebeebooks.com
bonnierpublishing.com

The Wonderful Habits of Rabbits

little bee books

The habits of rabbits are many, not few,

with plenty of things that they love to do!

There's frightening frogs
and discovering moles.

In spring there is smelling
the fragrance of flowers.

In summer there's swimming and lazing for hours.

In winter there's building
a rabbit of snow.

Of course there is hearing
with great rabbit ears,

and finding lost things
that were buried for years.

There's hitching a ride
on the back of your Pop.

One thing is for sure,
he has the best hop!

And when you get home,
there's hugging your mother.

There's chewing a carrot
and biting a beet.

And when there is music,
there's thumping your feet.

is saying "goodnight"
with a hug and a kiss.